Sir Isaac Newton in his
black and **gold** waistcoat

Tommy Brock in
his **orange** waistcoat

The gentlemen rabbits
in their **grey** hats

Sally Henny-penny
n her **yellow** stockings

Tabitha Twitchit
in her **purple** dress

Old Mrs. Mouse and her children
in the **turquoise** shoe

Peter Rabbit's
COLOURS

With new reproductions from the original illustrations by
BEATRIX POTTER

F. WARNE & Co ™

blue

Peter Rabbit's jacket
is **blue**

blue

"It was a blue jacket with brass buttons, quite new."
From *The Tale of Peter Rabbit*

Flopsy, Mopsy and Cotton-tail's
cloaks are **red**

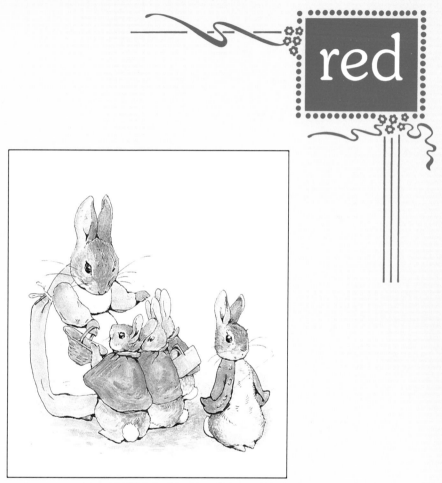

"Flopsy, Mopsy, and Cotton-tail, who were good little bunnies, went down the lane to gather blackberries."

From *The Tale of Peter Rabbit*

yellow

Sally Henny-penny's stockings
are **yellow**

"That's a pair of stockings belonging to Sally Henny-penny –
look how she's worn the heels out with scratching in the yard."
From *The Tale of Mrs. Tiggy-Winkle*

green

Samuel Whiskers' coat
is **green**

green

"Mother, Mother!" said Mittens, "there has been an old man
rat in the dairy – a dreadful 'normous big rat."
From *The Tale of Samuel Whiskers*

purple

Tabitha Twitchit's dress
is **purple**

purple

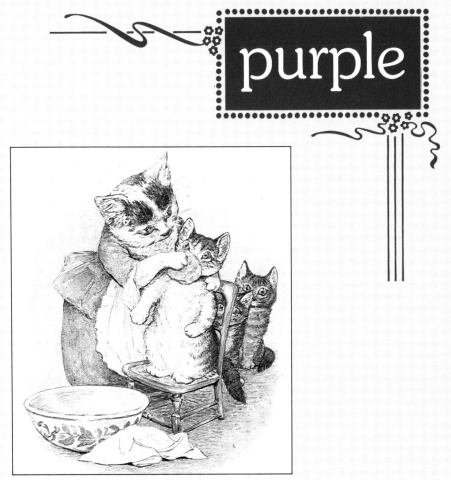

"One day Mrs. Tabitha Twitchit expected friends to tea;
so she fetched the kittens indoors, to wash and dress them."

From *The Tale of Tom Kitten*

Tommy Brock's waistcoat

is **orange**

orange

"Tommy Brock's clothes were very dirty; and as he slept
in the day-time, he always went to bed in his boots."
From *The Tale of Mr. Tod*

brown

Peter Rabbit's shoes
are **brown**

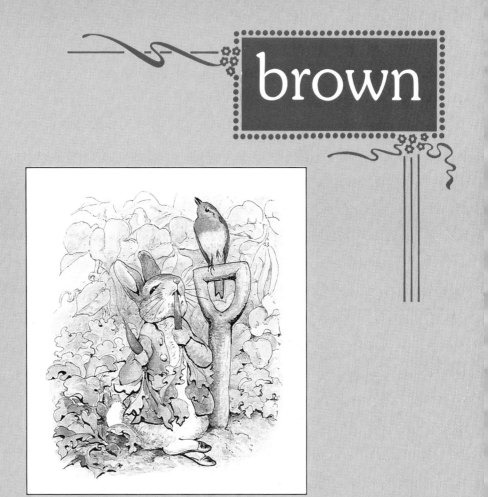

"It was the second little jacket and pair of shoes
that Peter had lost in a fortnight."
From *The Tale of Peter Rabbit*

pink

Miss Moppet's bow
is **pink**

pink

"This is a Pussy called Miss Moppet,
she thinks she has heard a mouse!"
From *The Story of Miss Moppet*

turquoise

Old Mrs. Mouse's shoe
is turquoise

"You know the old woman
who lived in a shoe?"
From *Appley Dapply's Nursery Rhymes*

grey

The gentlemen rabbits' hats
are **grey**

grey

Two gentlemen rabbits walking in the snow.
From *Appley Dapply's Nursery Rhymes*

black

Sir Isaac Newton's waistcoat
is **black** and gold

"His friends both came to dinner. Sir Isaac Newton wore his
black and gold waistcoat."

From *The Tale of Mr. Jeremy Fisher*

red

Peter Rabbit's mother's
pocket-handkerchief
is **red** and white

"Peter was sitting by himself. He looked poorly,
and was dressed in a red cotton pocket-handkerchief."
From *The Tale of Peter Rabbit*

blue

Jemima Puddle-duck's shawl
is **blue** and **pink**

pink

"She set off on a fine spring afternoon.
She was wearing a shawl and a poke bonnet."
From *The Tale of Jemima Puddle-Duck*

"Now I've finished my ironing: I'm going to air some clothes."
From *The Tale of Mrs. Tiggy-Winkle*

Mrs. Tiggy-Winkle washes and irons all the animals' clothes.

"And she hung up all sorts and sizes of clothes."
From *The Tale of Mrs Tiggy-Winkle*

Then she hangs them up to air.

Can you remember the colours?

FREDERICK WARNE

Published by the Penguin Group
27 Wrights Lane, London W8 5TZ, England
Penguin Books USA Inc., 375 Hudson Street, New York, New York 10014, USA
Penguin Books Australia Ltd, Ringwood, Victoria, Australia
Penguin Books Canada Ltd, 10 Alcorn Avenue, Toronto, Ontario, Canada M4V 3B2
Penguin Books (N.Z.) Ltd, 182-190 Wairau Road, Auckland 10, New Zealand

Penguin Books Ltd, Registered Offices: Harmondsworth, Middlesex, England

First published by Frederick Warne & Co. 1988
Reissued 1998
1 3 5 7 9 10 8 6 4 2

Additional artwork (details) by Colin Twinn

ISBN 0 7232 3551 1

Printed and bound in Singapore

Flopsy, Mopsy and Cotton-tail
in their **red** cloaks

Jemima Puddle-duck in he[r]
blue and **pink** shawl

Peter Rabbit in his **blue** jacket
and **brown** shoes

Miss Moppet in
her **pink** bow

Samuel Whiskers in
his **green** coat

Benjamin Bunny with the
red and **white** pocket-handkerchie[f]